DILLY
SPEAKS UP

by
Tony Bradman

illustrated by
Susan Hellard

VIKING

VIKING
Published by the Penguin Group
Viking Penguin, a division of Penguin Books USA Inc.,
375 Hudson Street, New York, New York 10014, U.S.A.
Penguin Books Ltd, 27 Wrights Lane, London W8 5TZ, England
Penguin Books Australia Ltd, Ringwood, Victoria, Australia
Penguin Books Canada Ltd, 2801 John Street, Markham, Ontario, Canada L3R 1B4
Penguin Books (N.Z.) Ltd, 182-190 Wairau Road, Auckland 10, New Zealand

Penguin Books Ltd, Registered Offices: Harmondsworth, Middlesex, England

First published in Great Britain by Piccadilly Press Ltd., 1990

First American edition published in 1991

1 3 5 7 9 10 8 6 4 2

Text copyright © Tony Bradman, 1990
Illustrations copyright © Susan Hellard, 1990

ISBN 0-670-83680-X
Library of Congress card catalog number: 90-70841

Printed and bound by Maclehose and Partners Ltd., Portsmouth PO6

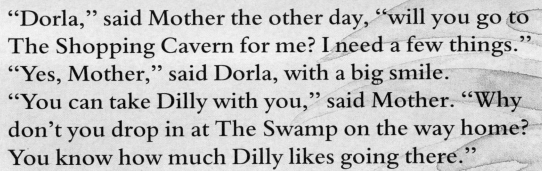

"Dorla," said Mother the other day, "will you go to The Shopping Cavern for me? I need a few things."
"Yes, Mother," said Dorla, with a big smile.
"You can take Dilly with you," said Mother. "Why don't you drop in at The Swamp on the way home? You know how much Dilly likes going there."

"I'll only take you to The Swamp if you promise to do what I say," said Dorla. "Now come and get ready like a good little dinosaur."
"I promise," said Dilly. "But I don't want to wear *that* coat..."
"Dilly..." said Dorla.
Dilly put on the coat.

"Dilly," said Mother, "I want you to be on your best behavior. And remember, Dorla's in charge. She has a list of things to do."

Dilly opened his mouth, but Dorla spoke first.

"He'll remember, Mother," she said.

"Good," said Mother. "Make sure you're careful...and Dorla, be home by 12 o'clock."

As they walked down the street they met
Mr. Darma, their neighbor.
"Hello, Dilly," he said. "Going somewhere
nice?"
Dilly opened his mouth, but Dorla spoke first.
"We're going to The Shopping Cavern," she
said. "And if he's good, I *might* take him to The
Swamp afterwards."

When they arrived at The Shopping Cavern, Dilly saw his best friend Dixie.
"Hi, Dilly," said Dixie. "Look what I've got..."

Dilly opened his mouth, but Dorla spoke first.
"I'm sorry, Dixie," she said, dragging Dilly away, "but
Dilly doesn't have time to talk right now..."

"One large jar of swamp worms, please," Dorla said to the dinosaur in the food store.
"Do you like sugared fern flakes?" he asked Dilly.
"I loved them when I was your age."
Dilly opened his mouth, but Dorla spoke first.
"He can't," she said, "he's not to eat anything between meals."

They had to go to the post office next. Inside, Dorla met some of her friends.
"So you're Dorla's little brother," one of them said. "Aren't you sweet!"

Dilly opened his mouth, but Dorla spoke first.
"He's not so sweet once you get to know him," she said.

At last it was time to go to The Swamp. A police dinosaur helped them cross the street.

"You look excited," she said to Dilly, who was bouncing up and down.

"And where are you off to?"

Dilly opened his mouth, but Dorla spoke first.

"He won't be going anywhere unless he behaves himself," she said.

But when they arrived at The Swamp, Dilly got a nasty surprise. "We don't have time to go in," said Dorla, pointing to the clock.
"Mother said we had to be home by 12."
"But I *want* to go in The Swamp," said Dilly.
"Well   Mother says I'm in charge, and you'll do what I say," said Dorla.
"No, I won't. I don't have to listen to you," said Dilly.
He opened his mouth...

...and let rip with a 150-mile-per-hour, ultra-special, super-scream, the kind that makes everyone dive into the bushes until he's finished. And when Dilly stopped screaming, he started to cry.

"OK, Dilly," said Dorla, who felt a little guilty. "You can have five minutes in The Swamp. I guess you have been good. But that's all."
Dilly had a wonderful time.
"I'm going to tell Mother you were horrible to me," he said on the way home.
Dorla didn't say anything.

"That wasn't so bad, was it, Dorla?" said Mother when they got home.

"Wouldn't you like to take Dilly out again some time?"

Dorla opened her mouth, but Dilly spoke first.

"Of course she would, Mother!" said Dilly with a smile.

He looked at Dorla...and they both laughed.